Reducing Your Foodprint

Farming, Cooking, and Eating for a Healthy Planet

Ellen Rodger

 Crabtree Publishing Company

www.crabtreebooks.com

Crabtree Publishing Company

www.crabtreebooks.com

Author: Ellen Rodger
Editor: Lynn Peppas
Proofreader: Crystal Sikkens
Editorial director: Kathy Middleton
Production coordinator: Amy Salter
Prepress technician: Amy Salter
Produced by: Plan B Book Packagers

Photographs:
Ellen Rodger/Plan B Book Packagers: title page, p. 20, 22, 28 (top), 29
Fair Trade Certified www.fairtradecertified.org: p. 24
Shutterstock: Laura Stone: cover; Dean Mitchell: p. 4 (bottom);
Selyutina Olga: p. 4 (top); Chee-Onn Leong: page 5; Diane
Garcia: p. 6; Maria Dryfhout: p. 7 (bottom left); Octopus: p. 7
(bottom right); kavram: p. 8 (bottom); Danijel Micka: p. 8 (top);
Muellek Josef: p. 9; Volker Rauch: p. 10 (top); Tish1: p. 10 (bottom);
fotohunter: p. 11 (bottom); PHOTO 999: p. 11 (top); Baevskiy
Dmitry: p. 12 (bottom); Paul Prescott: p. 12 (top); E.G.Pors:
p. 13; Teresa Kasprzycka: p. 14 (middle); Chad McDermott: p. 14
(bottom); Whitechild: p. 14 (top); Joe Gough: p. 15 (bottom);

Monkey Business Images: p. 15 (middle); Denis and Yulia
Pogostins: p. 15 (top), 16, 21 (bottom); Andrey Armyagov:
p. 17; Tyler Olson: p. 18 (left); Laurent Renault: p. 18 (right);
Lukiyanova Natalia / frenta: p. 19; Catalin Petolea: p. 21 (top);
Mark Stout Photography: p. 23 (middle); Serghei Starus:
p. 23 (bottom); Sandra van der Steen: p. 23 (top); Alfredo
Schaufelberger: p. 25 (top); Richard Thornton: p. 25 (bottom);
Dmitry Naumov: p. 26 (bottom); Zurijeta: p. 26 (top); JackF:
p. 27 (top); Veronika Trofer: p. 27 (bottom); Dino O.: p. 28
(bottom); Holger W.: p. 30 (bottom); thefinalmiracle: p. 30 (top);
Niderlander: p. 31 (bottom); Rick Oros: p. 31 (top)

Cover: Organic gardening is an environmentally friendly way to
grow your own food.

Title page: Farmers' markets sell fruits, vegetables, meat, and
baked goods, grown by nearby farmers.

Library and Archives Canada Cataloguing in Publication

Rodger, Ellen
    Reducing your foodprint : farming, cooking, and eating
for a healthy planet / Ellen Rodger.

(Energy revolution)
Includes index.
ISBN 978-0-7787-2922-8 (bound).--ISBN 978-0-7787-2936-5 (pbk.)

        1. Food--Juvenile literature. 2. Food industry and
trade--Environmental aspects--Juvenile literature.
3. Sustainable living--Juvenile literature. 4. Sustainable
agriculture--Juvenile literature. I. Title. II. Series: Energy revolution

TX355.R63 2010   j641.3   C2009-906924-5

Library of Congress Cataloging-in-Publication Data

Rodger, Ellen.
 Reducing your foodprint farming, cooking, and eating for a healthy
planet / Ellen Rodger.
      p. cm. -- (Energy revolution)
 Includes index.
 ISBN 978-0-7787-2936-5 (pbk. : alk. paper) -- ISBN 978-0-7787-2922-8
(reinforced library binding : alk. paper)
 1. Food--Moral and ethical aspects--Juvenile literature. 2. Diet--Moral and
ethical aspects--Juvenile literature. 3. Natural foods--Juvenile literature. 4.
Sustainable living--Juvenile literature. I. Title. II. Series.

 TX357.R544 2010
 641.3--dc22
                                                    2009048031

Crabtree Publishing Company

www.crabtreebooks.com   1-800-387-7650

Printed in the U.S.A./122009/CG20091120

Published in Canada
Crabtree Publishing
616 Welland Ave.
St. Catharines, ON
L2M 5V6

Published in the United States
Crabtree Publishing
PMB 59051
350 Fifth Avenue, 59th Floor
New York, New York 10118

Published in the United Kingdom
Crabtree Publishing
Maritime House
Basin Road North, Hove
BN41 1WR

Published in Australia
Crabtree Publishing
386 Mt. Alexander Rd.
Ascot Vale (Melbourne)
VIC 3032

Contents

Energy Conservation: "We Can Do It!"

"We Can Do It" was a slogan that appeared on posters made during World War II. One poster featured "Rosie the Riveter," a woman dressed in blue coveralls (shown below). The poster was originally intended to encourage women to enter the workforce in industry to replace the men who left to serve in the war. Today, the image of Rosie the Riveter represents a time when people came together as a society to reach a common goal. Today's energy challenge can be combatted in a similar way. Together, we can work to save our planet from the pollution caused by burning **fossil fuels** by learning to conserve energy and developing alternative energy sources.

We Can Do It!

WAR PRODUCTION CO-ORDINATING COMMITTEE

Eco-Awareness

Where do you think your trash goes after you throw it out? Making less trash means less of it goes to landfills.

The next time you are outdoors, do an eco-aware exercise and take note of things in your environment.

Just about everything humans do has an impact on the environment. Humans create mountains of trash everyday. They drive pollution-spewing cars. They use fossil fuel-produced energy to power electric appliances such as refrigerators, computers, televisions, and microwave ovens. It is difficult to live in the modern world and not be an energy consumer and a trash producer. The trick is to be aware of how much you consume, and how it effects the environment. This is the first step to being eco-aware.

Eco What and Why?

Eco-awareness means being knowledgable about the environment. It also means taking care of the environment. This is very important today when Earth's environment is in danger.

Climate Change

Another step to being eco-aware is acknowledging the part you play in the environment. Scientists believe humans are to blame for climate change and global warming. Global warming is an increase in the average temperature of Earth and its oceans. It is caused by excess greenhouse gases that are **emitted** into Earth's **atmosphere**. These gases, come from burning fossil fuels such as oil, natural gas, and coal as automobile fuel and for electricity. They trap the Sun's heat in Earth's atmosphere. The results of climate change include prolonged droughts, stronger hurricanes, and melting Arctic and Antarctic ice.

Global warming is causing Arctic ice and glaciers to melt at an alarming rate. This contributes to rising sea levels and animal and human habitat destruction.

Sustainable Living

Sustainable **living means meeting our need for food, shelter, and transportation** without hurting the planet or making it hard for people in the future to do the same. Human survival and well-being depends on the well-being of the planet. Sustainable living includes caring for the environment by not destroying ecosystems, or poisoning the air or land. It also includes caring for other humans or animals in the environment and making the world a better place socially and economically. As the world's population grows, our need for more food will grow and our use of fossil fuels is expected to grow too. Experts believe Earth will have seven billion human inhabitants by 2012. This means everything we do will have an impact on the planet, including how we dispose of our trash and how we grow the food we eat. Sustainable living practices include organic farming, **reducing the amount of packaged foods we eat, and conserving water and energy for the future.**

What's a Foodprint?

Farming, traveling, and eating have an effect on the environment. Almost 20 years ago, two scientists developed a way to calculate the human environmental impact on Earth. The Ecological Footprint method calculates how much water and land humans in a specific area need to produce all the resources that they use.

Many foods sold at farmer's markets are locally grown. You can check with the seller to find out for sure.

Measuring Your Impact

Today, there are many footprint calculators that people can use to determine their impact on the planet. Since some people use more resources such as fossil fuels in transportation, or through electricity use, their footprint will be greater than others. The goal is to make a footprint as small as possible in order to achieve sustainable living.

Foodprint

A foodprint is a way of calculating how your diet—the foods you eat and how they are grown and prepared—effects the environment. Like an Ecological Footprint, a foodprint takes into account how much fossil fuel energy was used to grow your food. It also examines how far food travels from farm to plate. A foodprint calculates the area needed to feed one average person. Foodprints vary according to where a person lives.

Foodprint Research

In 2009, researchers at Cornell University in New York examined the foodprint for the average person in New York state. They determined that the optimum, or best, foodprint is a balanced diet of locally-grown vegetables and fruit with about 2.2 ounces (62 grams) of meat or eggs per day. That diet could be followed with food coming from a 30-mile (48-km) radius of most urban centers. The researchers called the 30-mile radius, a "foodshed." They determined that the best foodprint diet would require 0.6 acres (0.2 hectares) of farmland per person.

Lessons From the Ancients

Potatoes have been cultivated in the Andes Mountains of Peru for thousands of years. The harsh mountain climate meant that the indigenous Inca people grew hundreds of different varieties on small terraced, or stepped, plots. Each square foot grew a different variety which was adapted to different weather conditions, pests, and diseases. If a disease wiped out one variety, there were many others that would survive. This meant that the Ancient Inca people could count on a crop of their staple food to feed themselves. The potato was transported to Europe in the 1500s, but farmers did not start growing them to feed humans until the 1700s. Most Europeans grew only one or two varieties. This practice of growing one single crop or a variety of the same crop over a wide region, is called monoculture. Monoculture crops are more likely to get diseases because all the plants are genetically the same and have the same resistence to disease. In Ireland in the 1840s, a devastating potato disease called blight destroyed the staple monoculture potato crop several years in a row. This caused a famine, where thousands of people starved to death or died of starvation-related illness. At the time, the Irish grew a monocrop of only one variety of potato—the lumper.

Hundreds of potato varieties were adapted to the variable weather of the Andes mountain terraces.

History of Cultivation

Humans began cultivating, or farming, crops for food more than 10,000 years ago. Before that, they spent much of their time hunting wild animals and foraging, or gathering, wild fruits and vegetables. Hunting and gathering food was difficult and never guaranteed success. Humans had to roam far to find enough food to eat. Farming crops changed the way humans lived. Crops take months to mature, so farming ensured that people stayed put, living in small permanent communities.

Wheat is one of the world's most widely cultivated crops, behind maize, or corn, and rice.

Wheat

Agriculture developed around the globe as humans learned it was easier to grow crops than to find wild plants on gathering expeditions. Wheat was one of the first cultivated food crops. It evolved from a wild grass and was first grown in the **Fertile Crescent** region of the Middle East. Wheat seeds were sown, or planted, by hand. Wheat allowed humans to make a variety of foods, but the best known wheat product is bread. Wheat quickly became valuable. It was bought and sold as a **commodity**.

Many rice crops in Asia are still cultivated by hand, they way they have been for thousands of years.

Ancient Grains

As cultivation spread, so did methods of farming. Different methods and tools developed to suit specific geographies and crops. In ancient China and Korea, farmers grew rice in paddy fields. Rice is a grain that needs a lot of water to grow. Ancient rice farmers terraced the land, and built canals and water reservoirs. The same basic methods of rice cultivation are still used today. From its origin, rice spread throughout Asia. Through trade, it was brought to the Middle East, Europe, and Africa. European colonizers brought rice and wheat to the **New World.**

New World Order

Many foods common to **cuisines** around the world have their origins in the New World. Corn is a food crop and animal **fodder** that was first cultivated in **Mesoamerica**. It only spread to the rest of the world in the 1400s and 1500s. Today, it is one of the world's most important crops. Squash also originated in Mesoamerica and tomatoes and potatoes are native to South America. Often, when crops spread from one area of the world to another, farming methods and cultivars, or plant varieties, change.

Conservation Tip

The next time you push the family's cart through a grocery store, look around at where the food is located. Is your family buying most of its food from the inner aisles where the packaged food is located? Is your cart loaded up with fresh fruit and vegetables, usually located on the outer aisles?

It takes more land to grow beef cattle and pasture milk cows than it takes to grow vegetable crops for food.

Large industrial or commercial farms often require a lot of irrigation water to grow crops.

Polyculture Farming

The ancient people often had hundreds of varieties for each crop. Each variety had a specific growing condition or disease resistence. They also grew several different or diverse crops in the same space or field. This practice, called polyculture farming, helped ensure that a crop would survive if struck by a disease because they are not all the same. They rotated crops to enrich the soil. They grew crops that left nutrients in the soil one season, so that another crop would benefit the next season. Some ancient farmers grew different crops next to each other to provide natural pest control. This practice is called companion planting. Polyculture farming is still practiced today on some smaller farms and in organic farming.

Monoculture Farming

Monoculture farming is a method of farming that produces a large amount of a single crop. Many **commercial farms** are monoculture farms. Today, monoculture crop varieties are bred to produce high yields. The crops are genetically similar or identical. Some are **genetically modified** to be disease resistent. Monoculture farming requires that the soil be enriched with manure or chemical fertilizers and **pesticides**. Over the last 50 years, monoculture farming has reduced the amount of land needed for farming.

Green Revolution

In 1945, a movement now known as the green revolution widened the scope of monoculture farming throughout the world. The green revolution brought new farming technologies such as chemical fertilizers to areas of the world that previously had only traditional farming methods. It increased yields and fed more people, but environmentalists say it created less diversity and more potential for disasters such as famines.

The green revolution brought agricultural science and chemical pesticides to the developing world.

CASE STUDY

What Your Great Grandparents Ate

It is likely that you do not eat the same way that your great grandparents ate when they were children. In the days before refrigeration, fast food outlets, and prepackaged foods, people cooked at home. Most homes did not have electric fridges until the 1920s or 1930s. Some perishable food could be kept in ice boxes, but mostly people ate food that did not have to be stored in a cold place. They also ate more food that was "in season." In season food meant food that grew locally. Eating food in season depends on where you live. In southern California, some food is grown throughout the year. In New York, apples grow in the summer. They are harvested, depending on their variety, throughout the fall. In your grandparent's day, apples were kept in a cool storage place such as a basement cold cellar, and if they were lucky, they lasted until the next spring. Once they were eaten, there was no more to be had until the next harvest. Fruits such as strawberries and cherries were only available fresh once a year. In northern areas, this meant June or July. Root vegetables such as potatoes, carrots, beets, turnips, and parsnips were harvested in the fall and kept in cellars until they ran out. Vegetables such as peas and corn were only eaten in season once a year.

Foods from Afar

Have you ever eaten a banana and wondered where it was grown and how it reached your grocery store? Many foods we eat today travel thousands of miles or kilometers to reach our plates. Bananas are tropical fruits. Many of those sold in North American stores are grown on massive plantations in Central and South America. They are shipped by truck, ship, and airplane to markets and grocery stores. Bananas are a high mileage food, meaning that they travel a great distance.

Food Miles

Food miles is a method for calculating the **environmental impact** of food by measuring how far it travels from the farm it was grown on to the kitchen it is eaten in. Often, a food item that travels a great distance uses more fossil fuels and creates more carbon or greenhouse gas emissions than a food grown locally.

Pesticides and Herbicides

How far a food travels is only one part of its environmental impact. Consumers also need to know how the food is grown. Did the farm use chemical fertilizers made from fossil fuel **petrochemicals**? How much pollution was created to grow the crop? Bananas require a lot of care to grow. Most non-organic plantation farmers use chemical pesticides to kill pests that feed on banana plants. Chemical **herbicides** are also used to guard against fungus and disease that harm banana plants. Bunches of bananas are sometimes even wrapped in pesticide coated plastic bags.

This truckload of bananas travels from the plantation in India to the shipyard where it is shipped to Europe. Once there, the bananas are off-loaded and trucked to distribution points and then markets and stores.

12

Global foods

Hundreds of years ago, traders sailed the world in search of exotic spices. These spices, including pepper, cloves, nutmeg, and cinnamon, were valuable commodities. Traders brought the spices grown in Asia to Europe, where people gained a taste for them and used them daily. Spices perfumed homes, made food taste better, and were even used in religious ceremonies. The early spice trade is an example of how a product produced far away became common. Early spice traders traveled on sailing ships, and rode camels or donkeys along overland trading routes. Today, people eat foods everyday that are not grown anywhere near where they live. We eat mangos grown in India, and chocolate produced in Switzerland from cocoa beans originating in Mexico and grown in Ghana. Our tastes are global because we have immigrated from all over the world and have brought our foods with us. We do not stop to think about how far the foods we eat traveled to reach us, or even how they traveled.

Cargo ships move products from one part of the world to another.

Making choices

Knowing how far food travels or how it was grown are important things to be aware of when buying and eating foods. Other things that might influence your food choice is whether it is fresh or needs refrigeration. Refrigerated and frozen foods use a lot of electricity. Foods grown out of season in greenhouses also use a lot of energy and can even be worse for the environment than the same food that is shipped thousands of miles.

Conservation Tip

The next time you eat a fruit cup or can of peaches, check the label. Where did that fruit come from? If the label says it was produced in another country, try to calculate that product's food miles by roughly measuring the distance from the country it came from to your home. Try using this web tool for calculating food miles: www.organiclinker.com/food-miles.cfm

Being an Ecovore

Do you know where your food comes from?

Ecovores tend to eat more local and organic foods. Some grow their own fruits and vegetables.

An ecovore is someone who shops, cooks, and eats with the environment in mind. It is a term first used by cookbook author Kate Heyhoe to describe someone who makes sustainable food choices that are as environmentally friendly as possible. Ecovore combines the words eco and vore. Eco is short for ecology, a movement that works to protect the environment from pollution and destruction. Vore comes from the Latin word vorare, meaning "to devour" or eat. Ecovores eat food that make ecological sense, such as organically grown produce and meats, and foods with a small foodprint.

Food Awareness

Ecovores make food choices based on their impact on the environment now and in the future. Ecovores do not eat food made from an endangered or rare species of plant or animal. They try to cook and store food using as little fossil fuels as possible. Ecovores also examine how their food choices affect other people. If a food is produced using workers who are underpaid or abused, ecovores avoid that food, even if it is cheaper than another food.

Foods shipped long distances by truck must be kept refrigerated. Fruits are often picked before they are ripe so that they survive the long journey to the market.

Diet Awareness

Being aware of what you eat can be tricky. It involves researching where your food came from and how it was grown or raised. It also involves how it was processed, or made into the final product that you eat. Generally, the less processed a food is, the more environmentally friendly. If the food you eat is packaged in several layers of plastic and shipped from far away, it uses more fossil fuels both in manufacturing and in transportation. Organic foods, or foods grown without chemical pesticides or fertilizers, are often healthier foods. They also leave a smaller foodprint because less fossil fuels were used to grow or raise organic food. A piece of local organically-raised beef is a better ecovore food choice than a processed hot dog that was made in a factory thousands of miles from your home. Reading labels on packaged foods is another way to be diet aware. It may not be possible to always eat fresh, local fruits or vegetables, but sometimes you can find canned or frozen versions.

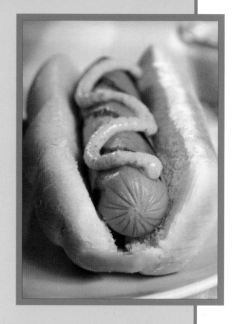

Hot dogs sometimes travel thousands of miles from factory to plate.

Reading labels can tell you what your food is made from.

Prepackaged and frozen foods are stored in petrochemical plastics. They often contain a lot of chemical preservatives.

School Gardening Projects

School garden projects are one way to learn how food is grown. Often, school gardens are planted to teach science, but gardens teach more than soil composition and how plants germinate and grow. Students learn math, nutrition, history, and most importantly, that food does not magically appear on store shelves. The Edible Schoolyard is a school garden project that began in 1994. Renowned chef Alice Waters worked with teachers, volunteers, and students at Martin Luther King Jr. Middle School in Berkeley, California, to turn a stretch of asphalt into a garden. The project fixed the school's unused cafeteria and made it into a kitchen classroom. It established vermiculture, or worm growing, and recycling projects. Over the years, the garden grew to include a fruit orchard, chicken coop, olive trees, an outdoor pizza oven, and even wheelchair accessible garden beds. Students work in the garden, seeding, weeding, and managing the crops. They learn how to save seeds from one season to be used the next season, how to cook, and how to look after the environment through simple food choices.

School garden projects teach students about how food is grown, how to harvest food, and what makes a nourishing meal.

Fast Food

Everyone knows about fast food. Full of fat, sugar, and salt, fast food is often fried and unhealthy. It is also tasty and makes up a significant part of many people's diets. A steady diet of fast food is a sure trip to poor health, **obesity**, and diseases such as **diabetes** and heart disease. Fast food is not healthy for the environment either. It uses a lot of fossil fuels in preparation and packaging, including plastics made from petrochemicals for containers, straws, forks, knives, and spoons. These plastics often end up clogging landfill sites and take years to **biodegrade**.

Slow Food

Slow food is a way of living, cooking, and eating that seeks to protect the environment. Slow food follows a food from its origins to its final destination on the plate. It is a **movement** which works to protect local plants, seeds, and foods. Today, the slow food movement has over 100,000 members around the world. A big part of its work is educating people about food and how it is grown. Members work to preserve **heirloom vegetables** and fruits and keep family farms in operation. They also lobby governments to enact laws against genetically engineered foods and the widespread use of harmful pesticides.

An occasional fast food meal is a treat. Eating fast food everyday is a ticket to poor health.

Conservation Tip

Do you know what you are eating? Food labels are one way to find out, but they are difficult to understand. Often the claims made on the box are misleading. Reading the nutrition label on the back of a package may be confusing, too. Watch for calories per serving size. You may be surprised to find a food that you thought was healthy really is not healthy.

Going Organic

Organic foods such as produce and meat, are grown without the use of synthetic or chemical pesticides and herbicides. Animals raised on organic farms eat organic feed and are not given **hormones** to help them grow faster, or **antibiotics** to fight infectious diseases.

Farmers who use pesticides wear protective clothing because of the danger of chemicals.

Why Organic?

Many people believe organic foods are better for our health because pesticide use has been linked to everything from cancer to birth defects. Pesticides and herbicides can also run off into water supplies, making drinking water unsafe. Antibiotic use in animals can also lead to antibiotic resistance, meaning that these drugs are no longer effective for fighting disease.

Organic milk comes from cows who are fed organic foods.

Conservation Tip

You can grow your own organic herbs in a flowerpot! All you need are seeds, good quality organic potting soil, and a pot that drains well. Plant herbs such as thyme, cilantro, or basil and keep the pot near a sunny window. When you harvest your herbs you can use them to flavor foods!

18

Farming methods

Organic farmers use old and new methods for improving the soil and preventing diseases and pests from destroying crops. One of the most important aspects of organic farming is polyculture. This ancient method of farming ensures a crop's survival by planting many different varieties or crops in the same space. Organic farmers also rotate crops to ensure that the soil is not depleted of nutrients. No-till farming, where fields are not ploughed or turned, is used by many organic farmers to make sure that topsoil and nutrients are not blown away. Organic farmers also use natural insect predators to keep pests in check. Natural **mulches** keep weeds in check.

Organic gardening uses the same principals as organic farming, but can be done in a backyard or neighborhood plot. Organic gardening allows gardeners to know exactly what goes into the foods they are growing.

Organic Labeling

In the United States, organic foods are regulated by the United States Department of Agriculture (USDA). USDA food labels on produce and packaged items help consumers determine what "organic" means. A label that says 100 percent organic means that the product only contains organically–produced ingredients. A label that simply says "organic" or "made with organic ingredients" means that 95 percent of the ingredients listed on the product must be organically grown.

Eating Local

A hundred years ago, most of the fresh produce and meat people ate was grown or raised locally. Spices, coffee, tea, sugar, and chocolate were imported from the mostly tropical and warmer climates these products were grown in. Today, most of the foods on store shelves travel thousands of miles. It takes a **conscious** effort to buy locally grown food. There's even a name for the people who buy locally produced foods. They are called locovores.

Grocery Stores

It is often difficult to buy local produce and meats in big chain grocery stores. These stores buy in bulk to save money. They get their produce from food terminals which bring it in from many sources, including big factory farms and foreign plantations. Grocery stores also offer a lot of processed foods such as frozen dinners, prepared and shipped from factories located many hundreds or thousands of miles from the store. Locovores purchase local foods directly from farmers, and from farmer's markets. Another option for locovores is food cooperatives, where many people join together to purchase larger amounts from local, and often organic, farmers.

Locally grown foods can be found at roadside stalls in rural areas and at farmer's markets and cooperatives.

Why Local?

Many people are eating locally grown and raised foods because it makes good economic and environmental sense. Buying local ensures that small farms can make money and continue to exist. This contributes to the local economy. Local foods do not have to travel as far and therefore contribute less greenhouse gases to the atmosphere. Buying from a farmer's market also allows you to talk to the farmer directly and learn how your food was produced.

Urban Harvesting

One interesting offshoot of locovore culture is called urban harvesting. Urban harvesting groups encourage people to gather wild foods, particularly fruit from abandoned trees in their neighborhoods. This fruit would otherwise rot on the ground. Urban harvesters also accept fruit from people who have backyard trees but cannot use all of the fruit themselves. Often, the fruit is donated to food banks or given to members of the harvesting groups who preserve it.

Urban harvesting groups give food back to the community.

CASE STUDY

Following a 100-Mile Diet

The 100-mile diet is the title of a book by Vancouver, Canada writers Alisa Smith and James MacKinnon. The book is a detailed explanation of how the pair spent a year eating only foods grown or raised within a 100-mile (161-km) radius of their home. They started their 100-mile diet after reading that the average North American eats foods that travel over 1,500 miles (2,414 km). Smith and MacKinnon decided to experiment with eating local and write about it so they could share it with others. They gave up favorite foods such as coffee, chocolate, mangoes, and bananas because those foods are from thousands of miles away. They found that they could eat a tasty and varied diet just by sticking with foods grown or raised close to home. Smith and MacKinnon planted a garden and canned a lot of their own produce. Most of their shopping was done at farmer's markets and smaller stores. Their book inspired others to attempt the same diet.

Green Cooking

Green living means living in harmony with the environment and caring for all of Earth's plants, animals, and ecosystems. "Going green" refers to a life style change where people change their behaviors and reduce their environmental footprint at home, work, and school.

Earth Friendly Acts

There are many things you can do to make your environmental footprint smaller. They include walking and using public transportation more often. In colder climates, you can lower the thermostat in the winter and wear a warm sweater instead. In warmer climates, you can make sure that your air conditioning is not running full blast. All of these small actions add up to less fossil fuel use.

Bake and shop green to reduce your cookprint.

Conservation Tip

When you clean up after yourself in the kitchen, try using Earth-friendly bio-degradable cleaners. These can easily be purchased in stores now. Remember to read the product label and check green living Web sites to find lists of green product ingredients. You can also make your own cleaners. Plain white vinegar is an excellent cleaner for glass, windows, and countertops.

Reducing Your Cookprint

You can be green in the kitchen too! All it takes is an awareness of
what you are eating and how that food is prepared and stored. Here's
a few hints about food preparation and cooking that can reduce
your "cookprint," or the amount of energy you use to make food:

1) When washing vegetables, fill a sink a quarter full and dump the
   vegetables in, instead of running the water. This wastes less water.

2) Avoid plastic or paper plates and forks and use dishes that can be
   washed and reused.

3) Buy and use only the food you need. A lot of food is wasted, either in the
   refrigerator prior to cooking, or as leftovers that nobody eats. Cooking a
   big pot of food and freezing some for later use is a green option, as long as
   the food is not wasted

4) If your family has a toaster oven, ask a parent to teach
   you how to safely use it and encourage them to use it,
   too. Toaster ovens are electric appliances that use less
   energy than regular ovens and can be used to cook
   smaller items, including toast or pizza.

5) Eat more vegetables (especially raw ones) and less
   meat. It takes more energy to raise animals than it
   does to grow vegetables.

CASE STUDY

Clean Your Plate

Have you ever had a parent try to get you to finish a meal by telling
you that somewhere, someone is starving? They were trying to get you
to understand that wasting food impacts more than just you. It is hard
to swallow something you do not like to eat, but have you ever thought
about how your waste effects the environment? It takes a lot of energy
to produce food from the farm to the plate. It takes
energy to grow the food, harvest or slaughter it,
and transport it to the food store. Energy is
even being used to cook it in your home.
Eating just one more bite is better for the
environment than tossing it in the trash.

Fair-trade Food

Some of the foods we eat regularly are imported from afar. Many of these foods, such as coffee, chocolate, and tropical fruit, are produced on big plantations owned by multinational corporations. This is not necessarily bad. Many corporations treat their employees fairly, giving them good working conditions and wages. Some are also environmentally responsible. However, some are not. It is difficult to know when you are buying a product produced by a company that respects the environment and its employees.

Fair-trade products are certified, so you know what you buy.

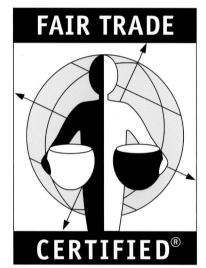

An Alternative

Fair trade is an alternative to buying products only from big corporations. It is a system that supports small scale producers and farmers. Fair trade gives farmers a fair price that covers their production costs and wages. Fair trade is considered a partnership with producers, such as farmers, and organizations which certify, market, and label their goods. A fair-trade label ensures consumers that they are buying a product for which the producer was paid a fair price and that no slave or child labor was used in its production or making.

Fair Trade and Footprint

Most fair-trade products travel thousands of miles from farm to plate. This means that their foodprint will be larger than more locally produced foods. They do not suit a locovore lifestyle. Many ecovores can justify their purchase because of the ethics of buying a product that directly gives back to the product's maker. Under fair-trade regulations, the environment is also important. Fair-trade growers use traditional farming methods that do not rely on chemical fertilizers or pesticides. They are often given assistance in naturally improving their soil and they are encouraged not to cut down rain forests. Yields are smaller but most fair-trade crops are grown organically. Products are shipped in biodegradable packing materials by sea, when possible.

Who, What, and Where?

Some fair-trade products are produced by cooperatives, which are farms or businesses owned and run jointly by its members. Each member shares in the cooperative's profits. Cooperatives produce foods such as coffee or chocolate, or preserved foods such as pickles and jams, and handicrafts such as clothing or jewelry. Fair-trade foods include sugar, rice, chocolate, tea, vanilla, bananas, coffee, olive oil, cotton, and even wine. Fair-trade products represent over $2 billion per year in sales. Most fair-trade products come from the Third World. They can be purchased at supermarkets and at specialty stores.

Buying fair-trade coffee is a way of supporting small farmers in other countries.

Fair trade invests in and helps protect the rights of farm workers.

Conservation Tip

Try to bring your own container of tap water for lunch. It is better for the environment! Tap water is treated and safe to drink. Plastic water bottles are a petrochemical product which use fossil fuels and must be recycled.

Alternative Eating

Imagine living in a comfortable home but pulling the ingredients for your supper out of a dumpster! Freegans, or dumpster divers, are people who can afford to buy their food from a store. Freegans prefer to salvage, or recover, perfectly healthy but wasted food from dumpsters. Freegan is a word that combines "free" with "vegan." Vegans are people who do not eat meat or animal products such as cheese or eggs. For freegans, dumpster diving is a political act that points out how everyone wastes perfectly good food. This in turn is a waste of resources, including the fossil fuels often used to grow and transport the food. Freegans take the food home, clean it, and cook it. Most of the perfectly good but trashed food they find is in the dumpsters of grocery stores and restaurants.

In some cities, freegans organize foraging and cooking nights to introduce other people to their way of life.

Conservation Tip

According to the United States Department of Agriculture, half of the food in the United States is wasted, yet over four million people go hungry. Are there ways that you can think of to not waste food?

Modern Foraging

Freegans also like to forage for "free" food in nature. This includes picking wild fruits and produce such as berries, nettles, and mushrooms. Foragers must be very knowledgable about the foods they eat, as some can be poisonous. They also like to plant guerrilla gardens on abandoned land. Guerrilla gardens are gardens that are planted, often overnight, on land that the planters do not own. The food planted in the gardens is tended, and at harvest, shared with the community and those in need.

Like guerrilla gardens, community and communal gardens are planted on plots of unused land. The difference is that community gardens are on public land, or on private land where a group of volunteers get the permission of the land owner. Foods are shared with the community.

Eating for a Better Planet

Vegetarians follow a diet based on eating plants. They do not eat meat, poultry, fish, shellfish, or products made from slaughtered animals. They do eat eggs, milk, cheese, and honey—products made from animals. Vegans are vegetarians who do not eat any animal product at all. Many people become vegetarians and vegans because they do not want to harm other living things. Some are concerned about the environment. It takes a lot more fossil fuel energy to raise animals than to grow plants. Some animals also add more methane to Earth's atmosphere. Methane is a hydrocarbon gas which contributes to global warming. Experts believe eating a vegetarian or vegan diet, or even a diet that includes some meat, but more vegetables and fruits, is better for the environment and for human health.

Vegans do not eat honey.

Making the Change

The foods sold at farmer's markets are interesting and varied. Try a vegetable or fruit you have never eaten before. You might be surprised at how tasty it is.

There are many ways you can help the environment through your food choices. You do not even have to make radical choices either. Each little step adds up to a giant leap!

Take Action

You can get your family or school involved in environmentally friendly food projects. Ask your parents if you can help them prepare a vegetarian meal once a week. Spend some time in your local library looking through cookbooks. You can probably find many easy to prepare vegetarian recipes that use only a few ingredients. You do not have to cut meat out of your diet, but eating less of it can be good for you and the environment.

Eat it Raw!

Raw foods are nutrient rich and they do not use up fuel for cooking. See if you can make a meal, or part of a meal, out of uncooked foods. This may mean eating raw vegetables as a side dish, or uncooked fruits for desert! Eat a varied diet. French fries for lunch everyday is not varied and it is not environmentally wise either.

Eat Local, If Possible

If your community has a farmer's market and you do not already shop there, ask your parents if you could go there on a family shopping expedition. You do not have to be a locovore to add local ingredients to your diet. Be aware of how your food was produced. Eighty percent of the energy used for food is used in production. Transportation sometimes counts for less than 10 percent. If your food requires a lot of cold storage to keep if from spoiling, a food shipped from further away could be just as good environmentally.

Shop at farmer's markets for fresh fruits and vegetables.

CASE STUDY

Community Kitchens

The Vancouver Community Kitchen project started in 1996 in Vancouver, British Columbia, Canada, to set up a number of community kitchens in the city. Community kitchens are places where people gather together, pool their resources, and make and share large amounts of food. They operate out of people's homes, community group spaces, church kitchens, community centers, schools, and anywhere they can get kitchen space. Often they use private donations, corporate donations, and government grants and loans to run. Cooking equipment is donated by businesses or individuals. By 1998, there were 25 community kitchens in Vancouver. A decade later, the Vancouver Community Kitchen project changed its name to Fresh Choice Kitchens. It began helping other groups set up community kitchens such as school kitchens. Fresh Choice also offers workshops on canning and community gardening. It even produced a cookbook that explains how to cook tasty, nutritious foods for 24 people or more.

Timeline

Food is one thing humans cannot live without. Over time, humans have hunted, gathered, and farmed food. The future of the world's food supply depends on how we treat Earth.

Spices are one of the world's earliest food commodities.

BC

Humans hunt and forage for food. Life is difficult and always nomadic, moving where food was located.

500,000 BC

Neanderthals discover how fire can be made to cook food.

17,000 BC

Ancient humans harvest wild grains and make porridges out of them.

10,000 BC

Wild grains emmer and einkorn are cultivated in the Middle East and northern Africa.

4000 BC

Ancient Egyptians begin making leavened bread and beer, using yeast.

3000 BC

Cattle are domesticated in Mesopotamia and Egypt and likely earlier in Asia.

100 AD

The Spice Trade brings spices from Asia to Rome and Egypt.

1492 AD

Explorer Christopher Columbus stumbles upon the New World. This paves the way for the introduction of new foods from the New World to the Old World and the Old World to the New World.

Christopher Columbus brought foods to Europe from the New World.

1700s

The potato, a South American food, is planted for food crops in Europe. Being a nutritious food, the potato improves the diet and health of Europeans.

1845-1852

An estimated one million people die and another one million flee Ireland during the Great Famine when blight kills the monoculture potato crop.

1860s-1880s

Massive cattle ranches are established in the U.S. states of Texas, Kansas, Nebraska, and Wyoming. Cattle are fattened and shipped to eastern markets.

1905

A Dutch scientist publishes a paper that noted "unrecognized substances" later known as vitamins, existed in some foods and were needed for human health.

1917-1918

When millions of men are called up to serve in the First World War, many are determined to be undernourished. This leads to research on nutrition and food science.

1939

Nutritionists in many countries work on war rations for World War II, developing guidelines for nutrition.

1940s

Use of synthetic pesticides for crops becomes common, starting the "pesticide era."

1960s

Organic farming, although not new, becomes popular among people looking for an alternative to foods grown with pesticides.

1989

The slow food movement begins and spreads to over 132 countries.

1994

The Flavr Savr tomato, genetically modified to stay fresh longer, is approved for sale. This ushers in the era of genetically modified foods. Due to the expense in producing the tomato, it never becomes profitable.

Cattle feed lots are crowded places. Small farms produce less, but animals are often treated better.

Flavr Savr tomatoes were changed to make them last longer.

Glossary

antibiotics Powerful medicines such as penicillin that destroy microorganisms that cause infections

atmosphere The layers of gases that surround Earth and absorb some of the Sun's energy

biodegrade To decompose or rot, leaving nothing behind

commodity A product that is bought and sold

conscious Aware and concerned about something

commercial farms Farms that exist as a business to make a profit

cuisines A style of cooking, often from a country or region

diabetes A disease where the body does not produce or process enough insulin, a hormone need to convert sugar and starches into energy

emitted Produced or discharged

environmental impact How something such as a human activity, effects the natural world

Fertile Crescent A crescent shaped arc of land in the Middle East where farming developed

fodder something that is fed to farm animals

fossil fuels Fuels found in Earth's crust that are nonrenewable sources of energy

genetically Something that has the same or a common origin

genetically modified A plant or organism containing genetic material that has been artifically changed to produce some desired characteristics such as long shelf life

herbicides A substance that is toxic to plants that is used to kill weeds

heirloom vegetables Vegetable varieties that have existed for hundreds of years

hormones Substances naturally produced by the body that regulate bodily functions such as stimulating growth

indigenous Originating or occuring naturally in a specific place

Mesoamerica A region of the Americas from Mexico to Honduras and Nicaragua where ancient civilizations such as the Aztec and Maya lived

movement A group of people who work together to advance a cause

mulches Material such as decaying leaves, spread around to enrich soil

New World North and South America

obesity Very overweight

organic farming Farming that does not use chemical pesticides and fertilizers

perishable Something that will decay or rot

pesticides A substance that kills insects that harm plants

petrochemicals Materials such as plastics or fertilizers, produced by refining the fossil fuels oil and gas

sustainable In ecological balance, or able to be maintained at a steady rate or level

Index